Angela
Nicely

For Sophie and Elizabeth ~ A M

For Jena and Elyse ~ D R

STRIPES PUBLISHING
An imprint of Little Tiger Press
1 The Coda Centre, 189 Munster Road,
London SW6 6AW

A paperback original
First published in Great Britain in 2014

Text copyright © Alan MacDonald, 2014
Illustrations copyright © David Roberts, 2014

ISBN: 978-1-84715-435-4

Printed and bound in the UK.

10 9 8 7 6 5 4 3 2 1

Superstar!

ALAN MACDONALD ILLUSTRATED BY **DAVID ROBERTS**

Have you read the other *Angela Nicely* books?

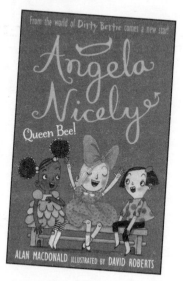

Coming soon…

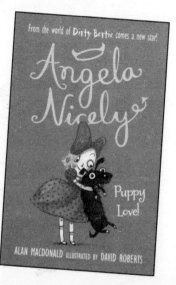

Contents

Chapter 1

Angela's class gathered on the carpet for News Time. This morning Miss Darling had some exciting news.

"As you know, it's nearly the holidays," she said. "So to celebrate we have decided to hold a talent contest."

Angela's eyes almost jumped out of her head. A talent contest? Yahoo!

"Anyone can enter," said Miss Darling. "Mr Weakly and Miss Boot have agreed to be our judges, and of course there'll be a prize for the winner. Who'd like to take part?"

Every hand shot in the air. Angela's was the first to go up. This was a contest that was made for her.

"Can we do any talent we like?" asked Tiffany Charmers.

"Of course, Tiffany," said Miss Darling.

"Then I'm going to do the dance I did for my ballet exam," said Tiffany. "I got a gold merit."

Angela rolled her eyes. Tiffany had told them a million times about her gold merit. From the way she went on anyone would have thought it was an Olympic gold medal.

At break time, everyone was talking about the talent contest. They only had a week to rehearse.

"I don't think I've got a talent," sighed Laura.

"You can go cross-eyed," said Angela.

"Mmm, I don't know if that would win," said Laura.

"I know," said Maisie. "We could do a pop mime! You know, with dance steps and miming the words."

Angela wasn't so sure. She'd already heard others in the class discussing a pop mime. "Don't we need something a bit different?" she asked.

"A pop mime *is* different," argued Maisie.

"Not if everyone else is doing one," said Angela. "I might do something on my own."

Just then Tiffany twirled past, bumping into them. "Do you mind, I'm trying to rehearse here," she sniffed. "So, ANG-ER-LA, what's your talent then?"

Angela shrugged. "I haven't decided yet."

"I know, you could be a clown," giggled Tiffany. "You wouldn't even need make-up!"

Angela ignored her.

"Anyway, it doesn't matter," said Tiffany. "It's obvious who's going to win."

"Who?" asked Laura.

"Me of course, cos I'm the only one with any talent!" smiled Tiffany. She shook her curly hair and danced away, pointing her toes.

"She's such a show-off," said Angela.

"Take no notice," said Maisie. "She can't win everything."

Angela sighed. That was the annoying thing about Tiffany, she *did*

11

win everything. She was class monitor, came top in every test and had been *Star Pupil of the Week* a dozen times. It would take something special to stop her winning the talent contest. The question was – what, exactly?

Chapter 2

After school, Angela found her mum in the garden rooting out weeds. She told her the exciting news.

"A talent contest? What a lovely idea!" said Mrs Nicely.

"Yes," said Angela. "I think I'll enter."

"Well of course you will," said Mrs Nicely.

"But what shall I do?" asked Angela.

Mrs Nicely threw another weed on to the pile.

"A dance?" she said.

Angela shook her head. "Tiffany's doing ballet. The dance she got a gold merit for."

"Don't remind me," groaned Mrs Nicely. "If her mum tells me about it one more time, I think I'll scream."

"That's why I need a good idea – or Tiffany will win and never stop talking about it," said Angela.

"Well, why don't you sing something?" suggested Mrs Nicely. "What about that lovely song you used to perform for me."

"Mu-um! That was at nursery school," said Angela.

"But I loved it, you were dressed as a teapot," said Mrs Nicely, singing the words.

"*I'm a little teapot short and stout,
Here's my handle, here's my spout…*"

Angela buried her face in her hands. She was never going to win the talent contest dressed as a teapot. Besides, not everyone liked her singing. Miss Crotchet at junior choir said her voice was loud enough to wake the dead.

Later, she spoke to her dad.

"Dad, what do you think is my best talent?" she asked.

"Ah, well, that's a hard one. You've got so many talents," smiled Mr Nicely.

"Yes I know, but which one's my best?" asked Angela.

Her dad thought it over. "I'd say your tickling."

"That's not a talent," said Angela.

"Okay then, standing on your head. That's definitely a talent," said Dad.

Angela nodded. It was true she could stand on her head longer than anyone she knew, but would it win the talent contest? No, to outshine Tiffany, she'd need something different, something special. On *Britain's Got Talent* they had all kinds of acts – a dancing poodle, a rollerskating granny and a man who could hippo-notize people.

Wait, maybe that was it! If she could hippo-notize someone it would be incredible. Maybe she could do it on Miss Boot and make her less cross?

"Dad, what's that hippo thing?" she asked. "You know, where you can make people do anything you tell them."

"You mean hypnotism?" said Dad.

"Yes, is it easy to learn?" asked Angela.

"I've no idea," said Dad. "I imagine it takes a bit of practice."

"That's okay," said Angela. "I've got time to practise." All she needed now was someone to practise on.

Chapter 3

Maisie and Laura were rehearsing in the classroom.

"I said left foot!"

"That IS my left!"

"That's your right, Laura!"

Angela came in and switched off the CD player. "How's it going?" she asked.

"Terribly," said Maisie. "Laura can't

dance."

"Not with you shouting all the time," grumbled Laura.

"Well, you can have a rest now because I need help with my act," said Angela.

Maisie folded her arms. "I thought you wanted to perform on your own," she said.

"I do," said Angela. "But I need an assistant, someone I can hypnotize."

"Is it dangerous?" asked Laura. "You're not going to make me disappear, are you?"

"That's magic," said Angela. "Being hypnotized is different, it's like doing things in your sleep."

"Laura will be good at that," said Maisie. "She's always daydreaming."

Angela stood in front of Laura.

"Watch my finger," she said. "Keep watching."

"I am," said Laura. "It's making me go cross-eyed."

She followed Angela's finger as it moved back and forward, back and forward.

"Your eyes are feeling droopy … ve-ry, ve-ry droopy," said Angela.

Laura blinked.

"You are falling into a deep sleepy sleep," said Angela.

Laura's eyes fluttered shut. Her head lolled forward. SNRRRRK! SNRRRRK! she snored.

Angela couldn't believe it. It was working!

"I did it," she whispered. "I really actually hypnotized her!"

"Now make her do something," urged Maisie.

"Laura, stick out your tongue," said Angela.

Laura stuck out her tongue.

"Say 'Eeenie meenie miney moe'," said Angela.

"Eeenie meenie miney moe," said Laura.

"Say 'Angela is amazing'," said Angela.

"Angela is a nutcase," said Laura.

"Eh?"

"HA HA! FOOLED YOU!" cried Laura, opening her eyes. "Did you really think you'd hypnotized me?"

Angela's shoulders drooped. For a moment there she'd actually believed that she could hypnotize people. This was going nowhere. If she couldn't hypnotize Laura how could she do it to anyone else? But wait … if Laura had fooled *her*, maybe she could fool an audience?

"That's it!" she said. "You can pretend."

"Pretend what?" asked Laura.

"Pretend to be hypnotized, like you did just then," said Angela.

Maisie frowned. "You mean you're not actually going to hypnotize anyone?"

"I won't need to," said Angela. "As long as everyone believes I've done it to Laura, it will work!"

"But wait, what if it's not me?" asked Laura. "What if you get someone else?"

"I won't," said Angela. "I'll ask for a volunteer from the audience and you can put up your hand. You just have to do what I tell you."

It would work, thought Angela, and what's more it would be the best act in the talent show – far better than Tiffany Charmers galumphing round the stage in a tutu.

Chapter 4

Angela waited in the wings to go on. The talent show was reaching the last few acts. So far the programme had included: Ryan's monkey impression, Dora's recorder solo, Tiffany's Sugar Plum Fairy dance and the terrible twins fighting each other on a judo mat. Laura and Maisie were on stage finishing their pop mime.

THUD!

Backstage, a door slammed. The Sugar Plum Fairy stomped out of the dressing room, followed by Amanda and Suki, who were also wearing tutus.

"Tell them, Miss!" complained Tiffany. "Tell them they can't!"

Miss Darling put a finger to her lips.

"Shh! What's the matter, Tiffany?" she whispered.

"They copied me!" grumbled Tiffany.

"I'm sure they didn't," said Miss Darling.

"No, we didn't!" said Amanda.

"But it's ballet and that's *my* talent!" wailed Tiffany.

Miss Darling sighed. "Tiffany, I think you should calm down and go back to your seat," she said.

Tiffany stamped her foot and stormed off. Angela raised her eyebrows. For once it didn't look like Tiffany was getting her own way.

Laura and Maisie finished their act and went back to their seats. The judges, Miss Boot and Mr Weakly, scribbled on their notepads.

"Thank you, girls," said Miss Darling. "Our next act is The Amazing Angela and her Hair-Raising Hypnotism!"

Angela slipped through the curtains. She wore her dad's jacket, a bow tie and a false moustache. The moustache was falling off and looked like a hairy caterpillar trying to escape.

"Thank you," she said. "For this act I will need one volunteer."

A dozen hands went up, but none of them belonged to Laura.

Angela coughed loudly. "AHEM!"

"Mmm? Ooh me! I'll do it!" cried Laura, jumping up to come on stage.

"Now I want you to look at my finger," said Angela. "Forget everything else – just my finger."

"I know," said Laura.

Angela began the hypnotism.

"You are feeling sleepy," she said. "Ve-ry, ve-ry sleepy. When I count to three you will fall fast—"

SNRRRRK! SNRRRRK!

Laura was snoring already. The audience giggled. Hypnotism was much funnier than they'd expected.

"Now, I want you to do what I say," said Angela.

"Do what I say," repeated Laura.

"Raise your right arm," ordered Angela.

Laura raised her left arm. Angela decided that was close enough.

"Stand on one leg," said Angela.

Laura stood on one leg, wobbling unsteadily.

"Now when I snap my fingers, you're going to dance," said Angela.

SNAP! Laura clomped around
the stage like an angry Sugar Plum
Fairy.

This brought the house down and
everyone howled with laughter –
except Tiffany, who sat stony-faced.

Finally, Angela clicked her fingers and Laura opened her eyes. People clapped wildly as Angela bowed low, losing her moustache.

"Very funny. Why don't you hypnotize me?" said a loud voice.

Angela looked up to find Tiffany had jumped to her feet.

"If you're so clever, why don't you try it on me?" she repeated.

"Um... Actually we don't have time," mumbled Angela.

"Don't be silly," said Tiffany.

Angela looked around in panic. This wasn't part of the plan. Laura was a good actor, but Tiffany would just stand there like a lemon. The act would fall flat – which was probably what Tiffany wanted.

"Come on, ANG-ER-LA, we're waiting," said Tiffany.

Angela stuck on her moustache. It was too late to back out now.

"Right, um, look at my finger," she said.

"I am – your nails are dirty," said Tiffany.

"Just watch my finger. You are feeling sleepy, ve-ry sleepy," said Angela.

Tiffany scowled. Angela had never seen her in such a temper. Her cheeks were pink and her mouth turned down. It gave Angela a wild idea. It was risky but worth a try.

"When I count to three you will become Miss Boot," she said.

The audience gasped. Miss Boot's eyebrows came together in a frown.

"One, two, three," counted Angela.

Tiffany put her hands on her hips. "Really Angela, DON'T BE RIDICULOUS!" she snorted.

The audience giggled. This sounded exactly like Miss Boot when she was cross.

"STOP IT! DON'T LAUGH!"
shouted Tiffany. "IT'S NOT FUNNY!"

This made the audience giggle even
more. Tiffany was Miss Boot. Her
face had gone red and it looked as if
steam might come out of her ears at
any minute. The real Miss Boot did not
look amused either.

"STOP IT OR I'LL ... I'LL ...
ARGHHH!" yelled Tiffany, stamping
her foot in fury.

"Very good, you can stop now," said
Angela, snapping
her fingers.
Tiffany stood
speechless as
everyone clapped
and Angela took
another bow.

"Thanks, Tiffany," she grinned. "I couldn't have done it without you."

The show came to an end and the judges met to compare their scores. Angela held her breath as she waited to find out who was the winner.

Miss Boot took the stage and waited for silence.

"In third place came Ryan, well done," she said. "In second place was Tiffany. But in first place was the act we all loved ... Dora and her recorder."

Angela let out a long sigh.

Laura patted her arm. "Never mind," she said. "Your act was by far the funniest."

"Definitely," agreed Maisie.

"Although I don't think Miss Boot gave you high marks."

Angela didn't care too much. She hadn't won but then neither had smarty pants Tiffany. In any case, there was always next year. Maybe she could borrow some of her mum's dinner plates and learn to juggle?

Chapter 1

It was a bright, breezy day and Angela's class was outside. Miss Darling wanted them to collect things for the Nature Table, which so far only had a few twigs and a carrot stick. She had split the class into two halves, with Mr Weakly leading Angela's group. He'd brought along his binoculars, magnifying glass and *The Pocket Guide to Bird Spotting.*

"Now today we are all going to be Nature Detectives," he told them. "What kind of things do you think we are looking for?"

Tiffany Charmers raised her hand. "Flowers," she said.

"We might see a butterfly," said Laura.

Mr Weakly nodded. "Good, what else might we find? Angela?"

"Bears and wolves," said Angela.

"Well, ha ha! I'm not sure we'll see any of those," laughed Mr Weakly.

"We might if they've escaped from a zoo," replied Angela.

Mr Weakly had met Angela before. She seemed to be a rather overimaginative child.

"Let's stick to smaller things like plants and leaves, shall we?" he said. "Why don't we all spread out and see what we can find."

Angela went off to hunt by herself. She didn't think she'd find anything very interesting on the school field. Mostly it was grass and mud. If she were Mr Weakly she'd have chosen somewhere more exciting to explore – like the Amazon rainforest, for instance. Think what you could bring back for the Nature Table – a snake or maybe a baby gorilla!

She poked around in the long grass. After ten minutes she'd found – a lolly stick, some dandelions and a soggy green tennis ball. They didn't seem like the kind of thing Miss Darling would put on the Nature Table.

Mr Weakly clapped his hands to call them back. "Well then, let's see what we've found, shall we?" he said.

"I found some leaves," said Laura, showing her collection.

"I got some seeds," said Maisie.

Tiffany was hopping up and down, desperate to speak. "Look what I found – a snail shell!" she cried.

Everyone crowded round to get
a better look at Tiffany's shell. Mr
Weakly agreed it was definitely
something that should go on the
Nature Table. He hardly even glanced
at Angela's dandelions.

Mr Weakly led the group through
the field to a gate and a small pond.
They poked around for a while, looking
for tadpoles or frogs. Angela fished
out some smelly bits of weed. She was
starting to think she didn't want to be a
Nature Detective.

Then she saw it – a footpath leading
away into a wood. Now *that* was the
place for a Nature Hunt. You might
find anything in a wood – birds,
squirrels, rabbits, maybe even a wolf!
There would be a million and one

things for the Nature Table. All Angela needed to do was persuade Mr Weakly they should take the path.

Chapter 2

Mr Weakly dipped a jam jar into the pond, filling it with gloopy brown water.

Angela crouched down next to him. "Sir, do you like woods?" she asked.

"Of course, a wood is a wonderful place to be a Nature Detective," said Mr Weakly. "There are all kinds of things to see."

"I know," said Angela. "And there's a wood over there."

Mr Weakly looked round.

"Oh, ah … yes, that's Thornley Wood," he said. "I don't think we can go there today."

"Why not?" asked Angela.

"Because, well … I told Miss Darling we'd stay on the school field," replied Mr Weakly.

"But it's not far, and you'd be with us the whole time," Angela pointed out.

Mr Weakly looked back at the school building. It was true that the wood would be the perfect place for a Nature Hunt – and they wouldn't be straying far from school. On the other hand, he didn't want to get in trouble.

"Please, sir," begged Angela. "Miss Darling won't mind – and think how pleased she'll be when we find loads of stuff for the Nature Table."

That did it. Mr Weakly would do anything to please Miss Darling. He pictured his group returning from the wood with armfuls of plants and ferns. Perhaps he'd even find some sweet-smelling flowers to pick for Miss Darling. He blushed at the thought.

"Listen everyone," he called. "We're going to take a look in these woods. But remember to keep together and stay with me."

Mr Weakly led the way, following the path into the trees. It was damp, dark and woody smelling inside. Angela felt they were bound to spot something exciting if they kept their eyes open.

"Now these trees over here are called oaks," explained Mr Weakly, pointing them out. "See how big and old they are? Who can tell me what an oak tree grows from?"

"The ground," said Maisie.

"I know, sir! An acorn!" cried Tiffany.

But Angela wasn't looking at the oak trees. She had found something far more interesting.

"Look at these!" she cried. "What do you think they are?"

The group hurried over to join Angela. She pointed to a line of tracks crossing the mud. The class stared in wide-eyed wonder.

"D'you think a rabbit made them?"
asked Laura.

"Or a badger?" suggested Maisie.

Angela shook her head. "Something
bigger," she said. "Maybe it was a wolf!"

Dora whimpered. Tiffany looked
round, in case they needed to run.

"Now let's not get carried away," said Mr Weakly. "They're probably dog tracks."

"But isn't that what a wolf is, a big kind of dog?" asked Angela.

"Well yes, I mean no… Look, I'm sure there are no wolves in the wood," said Mr Weakly. He could see that not everyone was convinced. "Maybe it's time to go back?" he suggested.

"Yes, let's go back now," said Tiffany. "We've seen the wood."

"No, we haven't," argued Angela. "And we haven't even found anything for the Nature Table!"

"Well no," admitted Mr Weakly. "Perhaps just five more minutes…"

He didn't want to return to Miss Darling empty-handed. Angela ran on

ahead, keeping an eye out for signs
of wolf tracks. Mr Weakly followed,
keeping an eye on the group.

Chapter 3

Half an hour later, they reached a fallen tree by a shallow stream. Tiffany flopped down on a large rock.

"I'm tired!" she grumbled.

"Me too," moaned Maisie. "When are we going back?"

Mr Weakly bit his lip. "Soon," he said. "As soon as we can find the path."

"I thought this was the path?" said Angela.

"Well, it's hard to tell," said Mr Weakly. "We seem to be a little bit … ah…"

"Lost?" said Angela.

Mr Weakly shrugged his shoulders helplessly. The trouble with woods was one tree looked the same as the next. He needed a map or a compass or, even better, a sense of direction. The main thing was for everyone to stay calm.

"LOST?" wailed Tiffany. "Are we really lost?"

"No, no," said Mr Weakly. "We're just looking for the path."

"But which way *is* it?" asked Tiffany.

Mr Weakly looked around him. All he could see were trees and more trees in every direction. To tell the truth he hadn't the faintest clue which way to go. In the hunt for animal tracks they'd somehow wandered off the path.

Tiffany was beginning to panic. "We ARE lost!" she moaned. "What if we can't get out? We'll all die!"

Angela rolled her eyes. This was typical of Tiffany. She was such a crybaby.

"We're not going to die, Tiffany,"
Angela said. "Not unless we get eaten by
wolves."

"For the last time, there are NO
wolves!" groaned Mr Weakly.

"But we did find tracks and they
could have been anything," said Maisie.

There was an uncomfortable silence.
Suddenly the wood didn't seem such a
welcoming place. They all looked about
as if a hungry wolf might be lurking
behind every tree. Mr Weakly swore
that if he ever got back to school he'd
never take Angela's advice again. Then
he remembered something.

"My phone!" he cried. "It's all right!
I can phone the school and tell them
where we are."

Tiffany stopped snivelling. It was

going to be okay. They would call Miss Skinner, the Head Teacher, and she would send a search party to rescue them. Mr Weakly punched in the number and held the phone to his ear. "Oh," he said flatly. "No signal."

There were groans of disappointment.

"This is all your fault, ANG-ER-LA!" grumbled Tiffany.

"My fault?" said Angela.

"You wanted to go into the wood!"

Angela scowled. If she was a wolf she would definitely eat people with curly hair and freckles.

"Now children, please don't squabble," said Mr Weakly. "I'm sure the path isn't far. Let's just keep moving."

He set off, plunging deeper into the wood.

Chapter 4

They walked and walked until finally they reached a fallen tree by a shallow stream.

Angela threw up her hands in despair. "Weren't we here hours ago?" she asked.

"Were we? I don't know," said Mr Weakly. He leaned against a tree and loosened his tie. He felt hot. The main thing was not to panic, he repeated to himself – or at least not to *show* his panic. They'd been gone almost two hours. Pretty soon it would be home time and parents would arrive to collect their children. Surely someone must have noticed they were missing by now?

Angela was staring at a tree. "Is that one an oak tree?" she asked.

"What? Yes – an oak tree," said Mr Weakly.

"It'd be a good one to climb," said Angela.

Mr Weakly sighed wearily. "We don't have time for climbing trees," he said.

"But if you climbed up really high, you'd be able to see," said Angela. "You could see right over the wood."

Mr Weakly blinked. Of course – climb a tree! Why hadn't he thought of that before? All they needed was someone who was good at that sort of thing. But who?

"I'm not climbing up there," said Tiffany.

"Nor me," said Laura. "It's dangerous."

"I'm a good climber," said Angela. "I can hang upside down by my feet."

Mr Weakly shook his head. They were already lost and he didn't want to risk someone falling out of a tree.

"No, if anyone is climbing trees it will be me," he said, bravely. "Hold my jacket and phone, Angela."

He stripped off his jacket and tie. He hadn't climbed a tree since he was eight or nine.

Ten minutes later, Angela and the others stood looking up. Mr Weakly was high in the branches above them. He seemed to be resting.

"Are you all right, sir?" Angela called.

"Um ... not really," answered Mr Weakly.

"Can you see the path?"

Mr Weakly shook his head. "Too many trees, I'd have to climb higher," he said in a shaky voice.

"Is that what you're doing?" asked Angela.

"NO!" moaned Mr Weakly. "I can't let go! I can't move!"

He had his arms and legs wrapped tightly round a branch. He remembered

now why he hadn't climbed a tree since
he was nine – he didn't have a head for
heights. As soon as he looked down,
his hands became sweaty and a wave of
dizziness swept over him.

Angela looked at the others. "Now what do we do?" she asked.

Maisie shrugged. "Leave him there and go back," she said.

"We can't just leave him," said Angela. "He might never get down!"

This was hopeless.

"Can you jump?" she called to Mr Weakly.

"JUMP?" he gasped. "Are you out of your mind?"

"Then you'll have to climb down," said Angela.

"I TOLD YOU, I CAN'T!"

Angela shook her head. Even if she could climb up, Mr Weakly was way too heavy to carry. There was only one thing to do...

"HEEELP!" yelled Angela. "HELP!"

To her surprise a voice answered back.

"ANGELA? IS THAT YOU?"

A moment later Miss Darling appeared through the trees. Angela had never been so glad to see her.

"Where have you been?" asked Miss Darling. "We were starting to get worried."

"We got lost," explained Angela. "We were following some wolf tracks but then we couldn't find the path."

Miss Darling looked at the children, puzzled. "But where's Mr Weakly? Isn't he with you?"

Angela pointed. "Oh yes, he's up there."

Miss Darling looked up. Mr Weakly's pink face blinked back at her from high in the treetops. He waved a hand, smiling foolishly.

"Mr Weakly, what are you doing up there?" asked Miss Darling.

"Good question, ha ha! I think I might be stuck," said Mr Weakly. "I wonder if you could fetch help?"

It took some time to get Mr Weakly down. Mr Grouch, the caretaker, had to come to his rescue with a ladder.

Meanwhile, Miss Darling took Angela's group back to school. Miss Skinner gave them squash and biscuits in the hall. She said it was probably better if their adventure in the wood was kept a secret.

Angela's only regret was that she couldn't show Miss Darling the wolf tracks. Still, at least she had something good for the Nature Table. It was a picture she'd taken on Mr Weakly's phone. It showed a big old oak tree, the kind that is perfect for climbing.

Chapter 1

Angela and her friends were on their way outside for morning break. At the end of the corridor they passed a small crowd standing round the noticeboard. Angela wondered what they were all looking at. She managed to wriggle her way through to the front to see. There was a poster pinned to the board.

SCHOOL FOOTBALL TEAM -
TRIALS THIS TUESDAY 4PM
Bring your boots!
Miss M. Boot (Head Coach)

Angela's eyes lit up. The school football team! Why hadn't anyone mentioned this before? Angela had never been picked for a team – not even for the Road Safety Quiz – but she liked the idea. If you played for the school team you might get your name read out in assembly. You might even win a shiny cup like the one Tiffany Charmers got for winning the Junior Gymkhana.

She tapped Bertie on the shoulder. "Tuesday. Isn't that tomorrow?" she said.

Bertie nodded.

"Come on, Angela!" sighed Laura. "Maisie and me are going outside."

But Angela was still staring at the notice. "I could be in the football team," she said.

Bertie grinned. "YOU?"

"Yes, why not?"

"You don't even play football," said Bertie.

"But I could," said Angela. "I bet I'd score millions of goals AND I'd be good at dribbling."

"Yeah, dribbling like a baby," said Darren. The boys all laughed as if he'd said something hilarious.

"In any case, you're a girl," said Bertie.

"So?" said Angela.

"It's a boys' football team," said Bertie. "For boys."

Angela frowned. "It doesn't say so on the poster," she argued.

"Look at the team photo – do you see any girls?" asked Bertie.

Angela shook her head.

"Exactly," said Bertie. "Anyway, you'd be rubbish at football."

"How do you know? You haven't seen me play," said Angela. "I might be super brilliant."

Football didn't look so difficult, she thought. She'd seen Bertie and his pals playing in the garden next door. All they did was chase a muddy ball up and down the lawn shouting "PASS!", "MINE!" and "IT'S THERE!".

Angela thought she'd like to be the player who scored the goals – the shooter or booter or whatever they were called. She'd be good at that – especially the bit where all your teammates ran up and hugged you.

Besides, they can't stop me going to the trial, she said to herself.

It was a pity that Miss Boot was in charge. Miss Boot taught Class 3 and when she shouted children covered their ears or dived under the tables to hide. Still, if Angela wanted to make the football team she would have to find a way to impress her. But first she'd need her parents' permission. Her mum was not keen on football. The last time Bertie's ball came over the fence it broke the greenhouse window.

That evening Angela waited until suppertime to mention the subject.

"You know tomorrow, Mum," she said. "Can you pick me up a bit later from school?"

"Oh? Why's that?" asked Mrs Nicely.

"Oh nothing, it's just I might try out for one of the school teams," said Angela.

Her mum looked up. "Really? How exciting!" she said.

"Clever you," said Dad.

"And what team is it? The spelling team?" asked Mrs Nicely.

Angela shook her head. "Not exactly," she said.

"Then what?" said her mum.

"It's um … the football team," said Angela.

Mrs Nicely practically fell off her chair. "The football team? Are you serious?"

"Good for you," laughed her dad. "I bet you'll be brilliant."

"That's what I said," agreed Angela.

"But Bertie says I'll be rubbish."

"Take no notice," said Dad.

"But this team," said Mrs Nicely. "It's a girls' team, is it?"

"Oh no," said Angela. "It's only boys at the moment – but not for long."

Chapter 2

The next day Angela called a meeting of
the GOBS club (Girls Only, Boys Smell).

"I've been thinking," said Angela.
"Wouldn't it be great if we all went?"

Laura opened her lunch box. "Went
where?" she said.

"To the football trial, of course," said
Angela.

Maisie groaned. "You're not STILL going on about that!"

"But it's not fair!" said Angela. "If boys can play, why can't girls?"

"Cos we don't want to," sighed Maisie.

"Boys are so rough," said Laura. "They push you out of the way."

"They wouldn't push ME," said Angela.

Maisie sighed again. "You're wasting your time, Angela."

"Laura will come with me, won't you Laura?" said Angela, linking arms with her friend.

Laura shook her head. "Sorry, Angela. My mum doesn't like me getting dirty."

"What about you, Maisie?" asked

Angela. "You're not going to let a
bunch of boys beat us?"

"I told you, football's stupid," said
Maisie. "Who wants to get all cold and
muddy?"

Angela puffed out
her cheeks. She bet if
it were a cake-eating
team Maisie and Laura
would be the first to
volunteer. And what
was so terrible about
a bit of mud? Angela
loved splashing through
muddy puddles in her wellies –
although not when her mum was
watching.

Still, she thought, Laura and Maisie
weren't the only girls in the school.

There must be others who'd like to play for the school team. But who? Not Tiffany Charmers – if it didn't involve ballet or ponies, she wasn't interested. Not Drippy Dora either – she burst into tears if you asked her to catch a beanbag.

"Why don't you ask the Payne twins?" said Laura. "They play football."

"Do they?" asked Angela.

"I've seen them in the playground," said Laura.

The terrible twins, Eileen and Myleen, were the biggest, meanest girls in Angela's year. The only problem was they'd probably boot *Angela* round the pitch instead of the ball. Angela sighed. If she wanted to get into the football team it looked like she was on her own.

Chapter 3

Miss Boot stood with her hands on her hips. She was wearing her bright orange tracksuit and a whistle on a cord around her neck. Sixteen boys stood waiting in a line for the trial game to start. Some were wearing Liverpool, Chelsea or Manchester United kit. Others were wearing borrowed shorts that looked like their granny's bloomers. Bertie's shirt was muddy before anyone had even kicked a ball.

"Now," said Miss Boot. "I have two rules about football. Firstly, I'm in charge and you play to my whistle. Secondly…"

She broke off as a late arrival came running on to the pitch. Angela was wearing a rainbow T-shirt, pink shorts and white ankle socks. Her trainers had silver sequins and flashing lights on the soles. The boys nudged each other as she joined the end of the line.

Angela Nicely

Miss Boot glared at her. "Angela, what are you doing?" she said.

"I'm here for the trials, Miss," said Angela. "Sorry, I don't have any boots so I'm wearing my trainers."

Miss Boot folded her arms. "You do realize this is a trial for the football team?" she said.

Angela nodded.

"I see," said Miss Boot. "Well, we've never had any girls before. Strictly speaking it's a boys' team."

Angela hung her head. Surely Miss Boot wasn't going to send her back to the changing room?

"Let her play, Miss. We don't care!" said Bertie.

"Yeah, it'll be funny," said Darren. "I can't wait to see her head the ball."

Miss Boot sighed and looked at her watch.

"Very well, you can play, Angela," she said. "I suppose there's always a first time. But don't expect any special treatment just because you're a girl."

Angela nodded. She knew Miss Boot would see sense eventually. Now to teach these snooty-nosed show-off boys a lesson. She would run rings round them. They wouldn't be laughing when she left them flat on their faces in the mud!

PEEP! Miss Boot blew her whistle and the game kicked off. She'd told Angela to play on the left wing. Angela wasn't exactly sure where that was but the ball

always seemed to be miles away. The
two teams chased it, swarming up and
down the pitch like bees.

THUD!

"PASS! Pass to me!" cried Angela.

But the boys ignored her. They
passed to their friends or else dribbled
in circles until they lost the ball.

Angela soon discovered why everyone else was wearing boots. Every time she tried to run, she lost her footing and slipped over in the mud. It was hopeless. After twenty minutes she had barely touched the ball once. Then came her chance. The ball was booted forward high in the air and came down just ahead of her. Angela dribbled it into the penalty area.

Suddenly she found herself with only Bertie between her and the goal. All she had to do was steady herself, take aim and score an amazing goal. The boys wouldn't be able to believe it. Miss Boot would say, "Well done, Angela, I'm making you captain of the school team!" The goal net yawned wide. She couldn't miss. Angela drew back her leg...

THWACK!

Something came out of nowhere and flattened her in the mud. Angela looked up to see the ball being hoofed upfield by a large boy with red hair.

She picked herself up, wiping mud from her face. It wasn't fair – surely that was cheating? She looked at Miss Boot, who shook her head.

"Well Angela?" she said. "Do you still want to play football?"

Chapter 4

The next morning, Angela sat down
beside Maisie and Laura. Her legs were
aching and she had a bruise on her
knee. Her mum hadn't been pleased
about her muddy PE kit. Angela had to
sit on a sheet of newspaper all the way
home in the car.

"Well? How did it go?" Laura asked.

"Did you get picked?"

Angela shook her head. "Boys!"
she sighed. "Who wants to be in their
smelly old team anyway?"

"Angela, could you come here,
please?" called Miss Darling.

Uh oh – what now? Angela trailed
out to the front.

"What's this I hear about you playing
football?" asked Miss Darling.

Angela shrugged. "It's okay, Miss,
it won't happen again," she said. "I'm
rubbish anyway."

Miss Darling frowned. "Have you
played much football?" she asked.

"Not until yesterday," said Angela.

"So you've never actually had any
practice?"

"Not really," said Angela. "I haven't

got anyone to practise with."

Miss Darling nodded. "Did you know I used to play football?" she said.

"You, Miss?" Angela stared in surprise.

"Yes, I played for Pudsley Jets. We were pretty good too," said Miss Darling. Angela's mouth hung open. She couldn't imagine Miss Darling playing football. She didn't look like a footballer – she wore shiny earrings – but maybe she took them off before a match.

"The thing is, you have to practise," Miss Darling went on. "It's like playing the piano. You can't just pick it up and expect to be brilliant."

Angela sighed. "It's not just that," she said. "I'm the only girl and the boys don't pass to me. But none of my friends want to play."

Miss Darling sat back and looked thoughtful. "Well, we'll see about that," she said.

At the next PE lesson Miss Darling said they were going to try something new. The boys would be playing rounders while the girls were going to play football. There were a lot of moans and groans from the class.

Tiffany blamed Angela.

"It's all your fault," she grumbled. "Why can't we do ballet in the hall?"

"Football's stupid," sighed Maisie.

"I hope I'm not playing against the Payne twins," said Laura nervously.

But soon the girls were passing the ball in pairs. They dribbled in and out of plastic cones. They learned how to shoot, aiming for the corners of the net.

At last Miss Darling announced they
would finish with a penalty shoot-
out competition. Everyone would
take a penalty and only those who
scored would stay in the competition,
until finally they had a winner. Laura
went in goal and saved the first three
penalties. Tiffany
went next and
toe-poked the
ball so feebly it
barely reached
the goal. The
twins, Myleen and
Eileen, scored
easily, as did
Yasmin and Angela.

After four rounds only two players
were left in: Myleen and Angela.

"Watch this," Myleen said to her twin sister, as she placed the ball. She stepped up and blasted it past Laura, but her face fell as it flew over the cross-bar.

Angela was next. She took a deep breath as she stepped back.

THUD!

Right, she thought. *I'm rubbish at football, am I?*

She ran up and thumped the ball with all her might.

It zoomed past Laura and into the roof of the net.

"GOAL!" yelled Angela, jumping in the air. "YAAAHOOOO! I did it! I scored! I won!"

"Well done, everyone," said Miss Darling. "After school next Friday I'll be running the first training session for Pudsley Girls' Football Team. Who's coming?"

A girls' football team? Angela's hand shot up. She looked around. The Payne twins raised their hands. Yasmin joined them and so did Maisie, Laura and half a dozen others.

"Brilliant!" cried Angela. They'd be Pudsley Girls United – and this was just the start! Wait till they took on the boys' team and beat them!